WALT DISNEY PRODUCTIONS
presents

The Mice
and the Circus

Random House  New York

Book Club Edition
First American Edition. Copyright © 1979 by Walt Disney Productions.
All rights reserved under International and Pan-American Copyright Conventions.
Published in the United States by Random House, Inc., New York, and simulta-
neously in Canada by Random House of Canada Limited, Toronto. Originally pub-
lished in Denmark as MUSENE PÅ CIRKUSBESØG by Gutenberghus Bladene,
Copenhagen.
ISBN: 0-394-84357-6 (trade) ISBN: 0-394-94357-0 (lib. bdg.)
Manufactured in the United States of America
      9 0   A B C D E F G H I J K

Inside the tallest tower
of Cinderella's castle
lived a family of mice.

The mice stayed busy
and happy.

But the mouse children
sometimes wished that
something exciting
would happen.

They thought it *was* exciting
when Cinderella and the prince
gave a big party or a fancy
ball.

But there had not been
a party in a long time.

One day, while the mice
were cleaning house,
exciting news came at last.

Miss Bluebird, who always knew the latest news, flew in the window.

"Guess what!" she chirped. "Timothy Mouse's circus is coming to town!"

The real name of the show was Dumbo's Flying Circus.

But Miss Bluebird knew that the mouse family thought of it as Timothy Mouse's circus.

Grandma Mouse had often told the mouse
children the story of how Timothy taught
Dumbo the elephant to fly.

The mouse children ran to tell grandma
about the circus.

"Please may we go?" they begged her.

"Yes, indeed," said Grandma Mouse. "We
will all go to the circus."

The next day the mice rolled out
the wind-up car to make sure it worked.
But they could not start it.

They pushed and shoved.
The car still would not start.
How would they get to the circus
without their car?

Just then Miss Bluebird stopped by again.
"Please, Miss Bluebird," said Father Mouse,
"would you go to Timothy Mouse and ask him
to help us get to the circus?"

Miss Bluebird agreed.

The mice stood at the window and
watched Miss Bluebird fly off.

She finally reached the circus grounds.
There were two tents and lots of colorful circus wagons.
Miss Bluebird did not know where to look for Timothy Mouse.

Miss Bluebird asked
the Tall Man if he had
seen Timothy Mouse.

Then she asked the midget.

She asked the
trained penguin...

and the clown.
But none of them knew
where Timothy Mouse was.

Then the circus
people took
Miss Bluebird
to see Dumbo.

If anybody knew where Timothy Mouse was,
Dumbo would know.
Dumbo and Timothy were very good friends.
But Dumbo was sound asleep.

"Maybe we can find Timothy without waking Dumbo," said the clown.

In a loud whisper, the circus people said, "One, two, three—CHEESE!"

Dumbo did not wake up.
But his hat began to wiggle.
Who should crawl out from under it but Timothy Mouse!
"Cheese?" he asked.

"I am sorry but there is no cheese," said Miss Bluebird. "We were just trying to find you. I need your help."

She told Timothy about
the mice in Cinderella's castle
who could not get to the circus.

"I will find a way," said Timothy.
"Tell them I will come for them tomorrow."

Miss Bluebird
thanked Timothy
and flew back
to the castle.

Miss Bluebird
told the mice
they would go
to the circus
the very next day.
The mice clapped
their paws and
jumped up
and down.

The next day...   the mice put on
their best clothes.

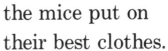

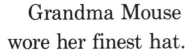

Grandma Mouse
wore her finest hat.

Mother Mouse powdered her nose.
At last everyone was ready
to go to the circus.

Grandpa Mouse looked at his watch.
It was time to leave.

But where was Timothy?

The young mice
climbed up to the
window to watch
for him.

Suddenly they saw
a dark speck in the sky.
"Here comes Timothy!"
they cried.

But it was not Timothy.
It was only a kite
flying in the wind.

The mouse children kept looking for Timothy.

Soon they saw another dark shape in the distance.

"There he is," they said.

But again it was not Timothy.

It was a big, scary owl instead.

The mouse children felt very sad.

They thought Timothy Mouse was not coming after all.

They thought he had forgotten them.

Suddenly a big
gray shape came
flapping around
the corner.

It was Dumbo—
with Timothy Mouse
in his hat!

"Step right up,
ladies and gentlemen,"
Timothy called out.

Dumbo stretched out
his trunk.
The mouse family
scrambled aboard.

"Seats in the rear!" cried Timothy.
The mice climbed into the square tent
on Dumbo's back.

Dumbo flapped his big ears and
flew high into the sky.

He flew very fast.

He flew faster than the steam engine
puffing along below them.

The circus was just ahead.

"Next stop, the Big Top!" Timothy shouted.

One of the
mouse children
leaned out too far
when Dumbo
swooped down toward
the big tent.

Father Mouse
caught him by
the tail and pulled
him back.

WHOOSH!
Dumbo flew right through
the entrance to the big tent.
The mice held on for dear life.
Dumbo flew up to the top
of a tall pole.

Dumbo stopped at a platform on top
of the pole.

"All out for the circus!" said Timothy.
"Best seats in the house!"

The mouse family hurried
down Dumbo's trunk.

The mice loved the circus show.
They watched the trapeze artists,
the clowns, and the bareback riders.

"And now," shouted
the ringmaster, "I have
the great pleasure
of presenting to you
the star of our show...
the one, the only—
Dumbo the flying elephant!"

From his platform high above the ground, Dumbo leaped into the air.

Timothy was tucked into the rim of Dumbo's hat.

Dumbo was wonderful!

He zoomed high...

and swooped low.

He balanced Timothy on his trunk.

Before he landed,
he even flew backward.

When Dumbo finished his act,
the crowd clapped and clapped.
The mouse family cheered, "Hurray
for Dumbo! Hurray for Timothy!"

After the show, Dumbo
and Timothy flew up
to the platform where
the mice were sitting.

It was time for the mice
to go home.

They told Dumbo and
Timothy how much they
liked the show.

Dumbo flew them home
in the moonlight, back
to Cinderella's castle and
their tower in the sky.

The mouse children were very tired
when they finally got home.

They climbed into bed right away.

"I think you have had enough
excitement—for one day at least,"
said Grandma Mouse.

"Yes, we have," said the little mice.

They fell asleep without another word.